Little Girls Are
Wiser Than Men

We would like to thank
UAEBBY and the Etisalat Award
for their support for this project.

ᘓ

First edition 2020
Tara Books Pvt. Ltd., India www.tarabooks.com
and
Tara Publishing Ltd., UK www.tarabooks.com/uk

Adapted from various translations
of the original Russian by Gita Wolf from
Leo Tolstoy's "Little Girls Wiser Than Men".

This book has been set in Monarcha, designed
by Isac Correa Rodrigues.

Design: Sanjana Vamadevan
Image captions: Divya Vijayakumar
Production: C. Arumugam
Letterpress-printed by T.S. Manikandan
and Venugopal at AMM Screens, Chennai, India.
Bound by M. Veerasamy, M. Vinodha,
M. Bhavani, V. Usha and P. Amsaveni

ISBN: 978-93 90037-00-1

Little Girls Are Wiser Than Men

Illustrated by
Hassan Zahreddine

Adapted from
various translations of the
original Russian tale by
Gita Wolf

SPRING PEEPS INTO THE VILLAGE.

It was an early Easter. Sledging
was just over. Snow still lay
in the yards, and water ran in
streams across the village.

A large muddy puddle had
appeared between two yards.

MALASHKA SPOTS THE PUDDLE.

Two small girls, from
neighbouring houses, found
their way to the puddle.

Their mothers had dressed
them that day in new clothes.

Malashka, the younger girl,
wore a blue dress.

The older girl, Akulka, wore a yellow dress. They both had red scarves on their heads.

The girls met, admired each other's dresses, and wondered what to play. What they wanted most was to splash about in the puddle.

The little one immediately started to walk into the water with her boots on.

AKULKA LOOKS PLEASED.

TWO PAIRS OF BOOTS BY THE WATER.

The older one said, "Malashka!
Don't! Your mother's going to
scold you. Look, I'm taking my
boots off — you should too!"

The girls took their boots off,
lifted their skirts, and waded
into the puddle together.

The water came all the way
up to Malashka's ankles.

"Oh it's deep, Akulka!" she said.

"That's alright!" replied Akulka. "It's not going to get any deeper. Come on!"

They came closer to each other.

"Malashka, be careful, don't **splash** me!" Akulka yelled.

Just as she was saying this, Malashka's foot plopped into the water ... and it splashed right on to Akulka's dress.

The dress was splattered, and **muddy water** sprayed into **Akulka's nose and eyes.**

MALASHKA MAKES A SPLASH.

AKULKA'S MOTHER TAKES A STAND.

Akulka looked down at the
stains on her dress and lost
her temper.

Shouting at Malashka,
she rushed at her with a
raised hand.

Scared that she was in trouble,
Malashka jumped out of the
puddle and ran away.

At that moment, Akulka's
mother happened to walk past
the puddle — and she noticed
her daughter's splattered and
dirty dress right away.

AKULKA GETS A TALKING TO.

"Naughty girl!
How did you get so dirty?"

"Malashka splashed me
on purpose!"

Akulka's mother rushed over,
caught Malashka, and gave her
a sharp slap across the back of
her head.

Malashka began to wail so
loudly that all the neighbours
heard her.

Her mother came out of
the house in concern.

"What did you hit my daughter
for?" she demanded.

One word led to another,
and a loud argument started.

MALASHKA'S MOTHER IS MOST UPSET.

THE VILLAGE MEN BARGE IN.

Hearing this, the men of the village jumped out from here and there, and began to gather in the street in a large group.

Everyone began to shout.
No one listened to anyone else.

The quarrelling turned into brawling, and when one man pushed another, a huge fight broke out.

Who knows where it would have led, and how it would have ended?

WHOSE SIDE ARE THEY ON?

GRANDMOTHER TRIES TO HAVE A SAY.

But at that moment, Akulka's grandmother stepped in.

The old woman made her way into the angry crowd of men, and tried to prise them apart.

They didn't pay her any attention, and she was in great danger of being knocked about herself when she shouted:
"Stop! Stop it, you idiots! Look there!"

She pointed to Akulka and Malashka across the road.

AKULKA FINDS A WAY.

While the women were engrossed in cursing each other, Akulka had quietly wiped the mud off her dress.

She had come out to the puddle, and picking up a stone, had begun to make a channel to let the water flow.

Then Malashka too had come out to help her, scooping out the channel with a small piece of wood.

While the men were busy fighting, the little girls had created a channel that led the water out, across the street, and into the creek.

They had thrown the piece of wood into the water channel and were watching it float away. As it moved on, they ran along too, on either side of the stream.

The two of them went right past the place where the fighting was going on.

MALASHKA IS GLAD TO BE PLAYING AGAIN.

THE GIRLS ARE FAST FRIENDS.

"See that? You fools dragged each other into a fight, God knows why! Was it because of these girls?" sighed Akulka's grandmother.

"Well, they seem to have forgotten everything! They're friends again, bless them! They're wiser than you!"

GRANDMOTHER IS EXASPERATED.

ALL IS WELL.

So what could the men say or do — except laugh, look at each other sheepishly, and make their way back home?

BOOK CRAFT

The linocut illustrations in this book were originally etched onto linoleum, then turned into plates and printed on a letterpress machine. We chose this method of printing because it mirrors the linocut process, and evokes the classical look and feel of books during Tolstoy's time.

The story of the book (as we recognise it today) and the story of the letterpress cannot be separated from each other. The invention of the letterpress machine made it possible to compose text from individual letters cast in metal, which was a far speedier process than carving out blocks of wood by hand. As a result, books could be made more widely available and accessible than ever before. This also led to the craft of compositing type and creation of standardised typefaces. However, as newer and more efficient forms of printing emerged, like offset, the use of letterpress at a large scale reduced.

The production techniques used to create this book, which was letterpressed on a 1965 Heidelberg press, work with both the possibilities and constraints of the medium. Digital files of the text and art are used to create plates that relief-print on to the surface of paper. This retains the tactile quality and minor aberrations that are intrinsic to the letterpress process.

LEO TOLSTOY

Before Leo Tolstoy was a celebrated writer, he was a student who struggled through his university days with his teachers dismissing him as "unable and unwilling to learn." Later, he came to believe that children would learn when they were given the freedom to make their own decisions, and that adults could learn from children just as much as they could teach them. With this thought in mind, he wrote this story as part of a series of fables that took inspiration from the actions of children.